THE SPORT
OF MY MAD MOTHER

A Play

by

ANN JELLICOE

'All creation is the sport
of my mad mother Kali'

HINDU HYMN

FABER AND FABER
24 Russell Square
London

*First published in this edition mcmlxiv
by Faber and Faber Limited
24 Russell Square London W.C.1
Reprinted mcmlxviii
Printed in Great Britain by
Latimer Trend & Co Ltd Whitstable
All rights reserved*

All rights whatsoever in this play are strictly
reserved and applications for performances in
all countries should be made to Margaret
Ramsay Ltd., 14 Goodwin's Court, London,
W.C.2. No performance of the play may be
given unless a licence has been obtained prior
to rehearsal.

THE SPORT OF MY MAD MOTHER

PREFACE TO THE NEW VERSION

The Sport of My Mad Mother was not written intellectually according to a prearranged plan. It was shaped bit by bit until the bits felt right in relation to each other and to the whole. It is an anti-intellect play not only because it is about irrational forces and urges but because one hopes it will reach the audience directly through rhythm, noise and music and their reaction to basic stimuli.

The play is written to be acted: nothing is put into words that cannot be shown in action. Very often the words counterpoint the action or intensify the action by conflicting with it. Most of the people in the play distrust emotion and haven't the means to express it anyway and they tend to say things which they think will sound good. But at the same time they betray their real feeling either by what they do, or by the very fact that they need to assume a mask.

It has taken me some years to understand that the play is based upon myth and uses ritual. Myth is the bodying forth in images and stories of our deepest fears and conflicts. *The Sport of My Mad Mother* is concerned with fear and rage at being rejected from the womb or tribe. It uses a very old myth in which a man, rejected by his mother, castrates himself with a stone knife.

We create rituals when we want to strengthen, celebrate or define our common life and common values, or when we want to give ourselves confidence to undertake a common course of action. A ritual generally takes the form of repeating a pattern of words and gestures which tend to excite us above a normal state of mind; at the climax of the rite the essential nature of something is changed (e.g. the mass, a marriage service, the bestowal of diplomas, etc.). This play proceeds by rituals because the insecure and inarticulate group of people who figure in the play depend on them so much.

I have always been dissatisfied with the last act. The play was originally written to a deadline, and had I had more time I think I would have discovered then the principle upon which I have now made the alterations. What has changed in the new version? CALDARO has become DEAN, CALDARO was originally conceived as a swashbuckling Neapolitan/American, he gradually changed as it became clear that GRETA needed a tighter, more conventional liberal/intellectual to oppose her. I used to think that the play was about the conflict between GRETA and CALDARO, and while this remains superficially true I find that, at a much deeper level, it is about the relationship between GRETA and CONE. The character of STEVE (FLIM in the earlier version) was originally slightly unpleasant, but STEVE should be the link between GRETA and the audience and the means whereby she may, perhaps, be controlled.

ANN JELLICOE

February 1964

6

PRODUCTION NOTES

The stage comes forward to meet the audience and there is no precise architectural detail to mark where the stage ends and the auditorium begins.

STEVE sits downstage with several instruments and makes sounds (not necessarily music) rough or sweet, discordant or harmonious, rhythmical or arhythmic. These heighten scenes of excitement and may also give the cue to action.

The verses or poems etc., should be chanted or distorted according to the needs of character and situation. They may be pointed or emphasized by STEVE.

True blue. In Act 2 PATTY refers to the colour true blue. When this scene was first written *Vogue* magazine had named "true blue" as the colour of the season. Where possible and suitable substitute the current seasonal colour to which *Vogue* has given its blessing.

CAST

STEVE

Dean, a young American

PATTY, 17 years old

FAK, about 18 years old

CONE, about 19 years old

DODO, maybe a girl about 13 years old, maybe
an old woman

GRETA, an Australian

The Sport of My Mad Mother was originally produced at the Royal Court theatre on 25th February 1958 with the following cast:

FLIM (Steve)	Anthony Valentine
CALDARO (Dean)	Jerry Stovin
PATTY	Sheila Ballantine
FAK	Philip Locke
CONE	Paul Bailey
DODO	Avril Elgar
GRETA	Wendy Craig

Directed by George Devine and Ann Jellicoe
Designed by Jocelyn Herbert

ACT ONE

Down behind a back street, a protected corner.

Enter STEVE, *a young man fairly tall and well built. Pleasantly and informally dressed with care and taste so that he is "with it" rather than "way out".* STEVE *doesn't fuss, he lets events flow round him, but there is something decisive about his manner and he looks as if he wouldn't let people push him around much.*

STEVE *brings onstage a drum, motor horn, triangle, cymbals, etc., which he arranges on one side of the stage. He speaks as he works.*

STEVE: (*striking the triangle*). Pure and clear, very low harmonic content—practically a pure tone. (*Possibly trying another instrument.*) I like playing percussion, it's not difficult and it's satisfying—(*a little amused at himself*)—releases frustrations. I don't do it professionally, this job's just part time. I'm not a musician but I do effects here for the—(*gesturing to acting area*). I'm here—to—well to have a look—I like seeing how things work, what life's got to offer, I wanted to see what there was to theatres and acting. (*Possibly playing as he talks.*) Everyone's vaguely interested in the theatre, not many people know as much as they think they do. I was in an electronics firm after I left training college—

11

made valves and cathode ray tubes.
They had a special training course so I know quite a lot about electronics. Now I'm with an accountant—I like figures—They send me out to the different firms and I go through the books and draw up preliminary statements. You get to know how a business really works when you go through the books; the figures mean something, they have something real behind them. That's what interests me about theatre: it's not real. I mean a play is just something that somebody has made up. And yet—I don't know—it's curious—anyway that's why I'm here, it interests me, I can sit here and watch and play. (*Possibly playing.*) I enjoy playing, oh yes, it's my way of relaxing, I like instruments, the way they're made and the sounds they make. But what I like most is the way music reaches into you. I just want to reach people I want to make them feel, and with music somehow . . . music communicates, it reaches into people and they can forget their brains, their intellects and the way they've been taught to intellectualize about everything, they can just let music happen, let it happen physically to them. (*He plays a little.*) Mmm. . . .
(*Enter* DEAN, *a young American dressed with a little more formality than* STEVE *but with an air of expensive relaxation, possibly he wears dark-rimmed spectacles. A good-looking, intelligent and sensitive man.*)
DEAN: As you go down the main road there's a side street running off—you see them all over London—the houses are small, two or three

storeys high with dirty bits of net curtain in the
windows . . . why dirty? . . . Why don't they
wash them? . . . Who's "they"? . . . There's a
little newsagent on one corner and an empty
shop boarded up on another—why empty?
Why boarded up? As you pass you can feel a
kind of dampness. There's an old woman
looking at you from behind some of those net
curtains: you can feel her eyes following you as
you walk on—not quite stabbing you in the
back but kind of daring you. Half-way down
the street there's an alleyway: there's ashcans
at the entrance and at the bottom the alley
seems to turn . . . why not old woman?—It's a
free country! You walk down the alley and you
wonder what goes on round the corner. . . .
(*Enter* PATTY, *17 years old, a pretty little
cockney girl with a lot of make-up round her
eyes. She is looking at a home permanent wave
outfit. Enter* FAK, *about 18 years old, built loose
and big, dressed in real flash clothes. He carries
a box which he sets down. Enter* CONE, *a little
older than the other two, careless of his clothes,
but they are essentially sharp and he looks thin,
small and tough.*)

PATTY: (*to the audience*). Have a good look. You'll
    know me next time.

FAK: (*bringing out a gun which he points at* STEVE).
    Bang! Bang! Bet that give you a turn.

STEVE: They got me.

PATTY: You look after your drum.

CONE: (*stopping the others with a gesture*). Hey!
    (*He listens.*)

FAK: Hear anything?

13

CONE: Thought I . . . (*Signalling* FAK *to carry on.*) No.

FAK: Wotcher! Bang bang! Fireworks. Ten bob a box.

CONE: Genuine atomic dynamite.

FAK: Cor what a blast. Bang bang.

CONE: Hydrogen! Plutonium! Uranium! You won't get them in no emporium.

PATTY: (*together*)

(*counting curlers in her home perm outfit*). One, two, three, four, five, six . . . six small ones. One, two, three, four, five, six, seven, eight, nine, ten, eleven, twelve. . . . Mind you don't hurt yourselves.

FAK: (*to audience*) Surprise packet.

CONE: Mystery bunch of big trouble.

FAK: Six bob a box.

CONE: Five bob.

FAK: Four bob.

CONE: No fooling, no kidding. Look what you're getting for your money. (FAK *and* CONE *open the box.*)

FAK: Aw shut up.

PATTY: Thirteen, fourteen, fifteen . . .

CONE: What!

FAK: No!

CONE: Unrepeatable!

FAK: Unbelievable!

CONE: Stick it up a car exhaust.

FAK: Rip off the silencer.

CONE: Burst a tyre if you're lucky.

FAK: Two and a tanner at Woolie's.

CONE: Atomic cannon! . . . And six king-size Chinese crackers—real fire—plenty big bang!

14

FAK : Just the job for a bow wow's wagger. Wham! Whack! Clack! Splam!

CONE : Packet of sparklers: let the kiddies blind each other! Did I say four shillings? I don't ask four bob——

FAK : I don't ask three and a kick——

CONE : I don't ask three shillings——

FAK : Two and a tanner!

CONE : Half a dollar! Reach the moon on a Jet Morgan sky rocket.

PATTY : There should be another big one, have I been done?

CONE : Hey! (*He listens, motions* FAK *to look outside,* FAK *does so.*)

FAK : No.

PATTY : Are you listening for something?

CONE : Please to remember the fifth of November. (CONE *sees something inside the box.*) Whow!

PATTY : Instructions read carefully.

CONE : (*throwing the firework to* FAK). Lamp that.

PATTY : Firmly wind strand to root of hair . . .

FAK : There's gunpowder here.

PATTY : Thoroughly moisten with cotton wool dipped in wave lotion . . .

FAK : This'll give us a giggle.

PATTY : It must be strong, it don't half pong.

FAK : And uncle was going to raffle it. . . . Here, catch!

CONE : Catch!

FAK : Catch!

PATTY : Do you mind, I'm trying to read.

CONE : She's reading! Ah hah! What you doing, Patty?

FAK : What you doing, Patty?

CONE: What you doing, Patty?

PATTY: Aw shut up.

CONE: She's reading.

FAK: What'll Greta say to this, eh? What'll she say to this?

PATTY: (irritated). Aw Greta!

FAK: (teasing her). Aw Greta! Greta! Greta!

PATTY: Aw Greta! Greta! Greta! Greta!
(CONE laughs and goes and looks outside.)

PATTY: What you got there? . . . Well?

FAK: Something'll take the curl out of your hair.

PATTY: Where'd you nick it?

FAK: Hah hah.

PATTY: Bet there wasn't a copper for miles.

FAK: Couldn't bloody matter.

PATTY: Blow up Buckingham Palace! Oh no. Might upset Greta.

FAK: Aw shut up.

PATTY: Bet you bought it.

FAK: What?

PATTY: Bought it I betcher.

FAK: Wet, she says we're wet.

CONE: Nothing doing, Patty?

FAK: Slack Alice?

PATTY: Look to yourself, Faky-boy.

CONE: Look to yourself, Faky-boy.

FAK: Look to yourself, Faky-boy.

CONE: Seen you somewhere.

FAK: Somewhere before.

PATTY: Big act.

CONE: Sweetie peetie Patty-paws. Beat! Beat!

FAK: Going my way?

PATTY: Catch me——

CONE: Catch me.

16

FAK : Catch me.

CONE : Catch me, Patty-paws, who'd ever have thought?

PATTY : Oh, give over.

CONE : Give over.

FAK : Give over.

PATTY : Give over. Give over.

CONE : Give over, sweetheart.

FAK : Lovey dovey, night night.

PATTY : Leave me be, I never!

CONE : She never.

FAK : She never ever.

CONE : She never ever what?

FAK : What did she never ever?

CONE : She never ever been with nobody—what, nobody? No! No! No! Nobody.

PATTY : Stop it! Stop it!

CONE & If you see a big fat woman.

FAK : Standing on a corner humming.
That's fat Jessie.

PATTY : Is that so.

CONE & If you see her in the pictures

FAK : With a bag of dolly mixtures
That's fat Jessie.

PATTY : Is that so.

CONE & If you see her in a shop.

FAK : Sobbing on a great big mop.
That's fat Jessie.

FAK : (*bringing out his gun*). Yah!
(PATTY *screams*.)

FAK : Always scares birds.

CONE : Shut up. (*Listening*.)

PATTY : What?

CONE : Be quiet.

17

PATTY: You expecting someone? . . . Who? . . . Who!
Who!

CONE: Shut up. . . . Where d'you nobble it?

FAK: My Dad. He knocked it off a Jerry depot in
the war. Got a lovely axe but he had to chuck
it away. Plenty of ammo too.

PATTY: You want to be careful.

FAK: Kill a feller easy.

PATTY: Put it away, you soppy thing. You're talking
silly.

FAK: Don't you lip me! Don't you lip me like that!

PATTY: You'll get hung.

FAK: That's for stupid fellers. That's for stupid
fellers.

CONE: Relax. . . . Hands is quieter . . . see . . . there's
a spot there—just there (CONE *demonstrates on
the base of* FAK'*s skull*) and you hit—so.

FAK: Here go easy. . . . There?

CONE: Just there.

FAK: There.

CONE: Stick to the gum, chum. This requires finesse.
. . . Better keep it from—she don't like raw
gats.

FAK: (*uncertain*). Oh, I dunno, I dunno.
(PATTY *laughs and taking some nail varnish from
her handbag starts to paint her nails.*)

PATTY: Was I with you lot Friday week?

FAK: Went to the flicks.

PATTY: Friday before that.

CONE: Went to the dogs.

FAK: That's right. There was a shell-out and us and
some of the fellers went to the dogs.

PATTY: Ah . . . that's when Maureen did my hair.

CONE: How d'you keep your nails so long?

18

FAK : She never washes up.

PATTY : Don't be daft.

FAK : Nice smell.

CONE : Give me that. I'll do it a sight better than you.
(*To* FAK *indicating the exit*) Keep yourself
awake.

(CONE *paints* PATTY'*s nails*.)

CONE : (*whistling through his teeth*).
Bang bang bang and bish bish bish
Bang bang bang and cosh cosh cosh
Aldgate pump it ain't what it used to be
Poor old Aldgate pump. O!

PATTY : I never seen that blond feller since.

FAK : What feller?

PATTY : Since we went to the pictures with him—you
know, the tall feller, blond and quite good
looking really. . . . What happened to him?

CONE :·What happened to who?

PATTY : The feller I was sitting by . . . what was his
name?

CONE : Didn't go with no one else.

PATTY : Are you potty? He sat between me and you :
Fak then me then him then—Garry—Garry,
um, Garry . . .

CONE : (*jabbing her hand*). Shut up.

PATTY : Oo! Mind my nails. That hurt. . . . My Ma'd
slay me if she caught me with this on!

FAK : Go on, bet you beat her.

PATTY : Could be.

FAK : What's stopping you going off on your own?

PATTY : Oh . . .

FAK : Scared?

PATTY : What me?—I wouldn't like to live on my own,
that's all.

19

FAK: Why live on your own?

PATTY: Eh?

CONE: Are you not the flipping virgin.

PATTY: You keep your gob straight. . . . I couldn't, I can't, . . . I'll not be another Connie.

CONE: Eh? . . . Did you leak?

FAK: Yes, I told her and I told her to keep her mouth shut.

PATTY: I haven't told anybody.

CONE: Get this: It won't be me that'll be at you if you do.

PATTY: I've said I haven't told anybody, haven't I?

FAK: And don't you neither.

PATTY: I haven't.

CONE: Keep still . . . just remember: it won't be me.

PATTY: . . . Any day, any time of day, any night . . . in the streets, or the flicks or an espresso . . . (CONE *laughs gently*.)

FAK: Bet I can hit that harder than you. Bet I can hit it so it falls down.

PATTY: You'll break your fist.

FAK: Bet I can hit so——

CONE: Quiet!

PATTY: What you listening for?

CONE: Shut up! (*Listening.*)

PATTY: What! What's happened? Has something happened?

CONE: Aw sit down and keep still. I haven't finished yet..

PATTY: Well has it?

CONE: Has what?

PATTY: I don't know.

CONE: Well, what you flapping about?

FAK: (*hitting the wall*). They're yeller! They're yeller!

20

Ha ha! Bang! Bang! Bang! Bang!

PATTY: Aw shut up.

FAK: Bang! Bang!

CONE: You keep over there. (*Indicating the exit.*)

FAK: Why don't you take a turn?

CONE: I'm busy.

PATTY: Tell us about her and Ronny.

FAK: I told you that.

PATTY: Tell me again.

CONE: For crying out loud.

FAK: She had it in for Ronny so he hid himself and she let him. But she knew where he was and he knew she knew.

CONE: (*lyrical sarcastic*). And she knew he knew she knew.

FAK: And he knew if he stepped out he'd get trod on.

PATTY: And he had to, didn't he? He just had to. He got all sort of excited and dreamy of the thought of it and he couldn't stop himself. He had to—come out. . . . And she saw to it. She fixed it. I bet it give you kicks. I bet he had kicks in there just waiting and dreaming. I bet he got all worked up.

(CONE *laughs quietly.*)

I wish I was—I wish I was Greta. Greta! . . . Like spit on a hot plate that's her. Razzle dazzle. It's like—it's like she hits 'em and heps 'em. Anyone'll do anything for her. She'll have Solly caper down Blackpool pier with no clothes on and bash a copper with a Pepsi-Cola bottle. It's like she makes something come busting out. Everyone's got something inside and she makes it grow and grow and come

21

busting out. She looks at Solly. Solly fights
Bobby and first thing they know they're down
the end of the street fighting anyone they see.
And she picks them up and chucks them round
her head and that four is fighting eight and the
eight's fighting sixteen: the whole street's
fighting. It'll start with one fight and then the
whole street—all exploding and growing and
exploding, and every bit of every explosion
makes everything round it explode. The whole
street's fighting—the whole block—the whole
country—the sea—the air—all the planets. And
she stands there, her eyes glittering and
sparkling and laughing the whole time. Bearing
it. Bearing it.

CONE: (*painting his finger-nail*). Cute ain't it.

PATTY: O! Let's go somewhere. Get something started.
. . . It's Guy Fawkes. It's Guy Fawkes. . . . I
never been on a bash. I want—I want to know!
It's Guy Fawkes. . . . You'd do it for her. . . .
(FAK *and* CONE *exchange glances.*)
Is it . . . is it . . . her . . . eh?

FAK: Sort of.

PATTY: Ha ha her! Her!

FAK: Aw shut up.

PATTY: Ha ha! A game eh? What a joke. Oh men! Oh
men like being fooled. You men! You men!
Men! Ha ha! You men are in for a joke you
are! A surprise! A surprise!

FAK: Eh?

PATTY: Tell me, Faky—why you like eh?

CONE: Who says he likes her?

PATTY: She sends you doesn't she? She really sends
you.

22

FAK: Aw shut up.

PATTY: You'd do anything for her—anything.

FAK: Shut up! Shut up!

CONE: Hark, louse. I love you.

FAK: Shut up!

PATTY: Shut up shut up says Faky-white-with-fear.

FAK: I'm not afraid of her.

CONE: You're jealous.

PATTY: Jealous! Jealous! Me! You're all—no minds of your own. Men! My stars! Jealous! And she's not even clean. Men! And she has the lot of you—the lot—Harrow Road—the lot! And all for someone who's—for a woman who's——

CONE: Sweet feminine bitch.

PATTY: You said . . . you said . . . you said—she's not nice.

FAK: What!

PATTY: You did.

FAK: I didn't.

CONE: She ain't nice.

FAK: She is.

PATTY: She isn't.

FAK: She is.

PATTY: You say she isn't.

CONE: Spare me.

PATTY: And I don't understand you and I never will. You. You and all the others! All the others! What about them?

FAK: What?

PATTY: What about them. What about them.

CONE: What about them?

PATTY: The gang. The gang.

CONE: (*mocking*). The gang! The gang!

PATTY: The gang! The gang! The gang she runs! She

23

runs the protection! Pay up or squeeze! Break
your windows break your bones! Pay up or
scream!

CONE: Shut up.

PATTY: Aw! Greta'll hear! Greta! Greta! Greta! And
the joke—the joke! Ha ha! Hop! Hop! But
you'll soon see! You'll see! . . .

CONE: Quiet. Listen. (*Trying to hear something
outside.*)

PATTY: Changing isn't she? Changing!

CONE: (*to* FAK). Stop her. Clout her.

PATTY: Listening for Greta? Looking for Greta, eh?
Why's she not here, eh? Changed! She's
different! And it's going to get worse. Worse.
Bah! Mummy's boy Master Coney! Doesn't
love him any more! She! She! She's losing
interest and especially in Master Coney!
(CONE *turns on her.*)
. . . I . . . I . . .

FAK: (*inarticulate, trying to distract* CONE). Ah.

CONE: Eh?

FAK: . . . Dolly.

CONE: Dolly?

FAK: Dolly!

CONE: *Dolly?*

FAK: Dolly.
(CONE *turns to* PATTY *again.* FAK *goes to her
other side and by his desperation draws* CONE's
attention beyond her.)
Dolly! Dolly!

CONE: Dolly?

FAK: Dolly!

CONE: Dolly!

FAK: Dolly.

24

CONE: Dolly.
  FAK: Dolly.
       (CONE *and* FAK *have hypnotized each other.*
       PATTY *tries to get away and in so doing draws*
       them on to her.)
  FAK: (*at* PATTY). Dolly.
 CONE: (*at* PATTY). Dolly.
  FAK: Dolly.
 CONE: Dolly.
  FAK: Dolly.
PATTY: Shoo.
  FAK: Shoo.
PATTY: Shoo.
 CONE: Shoo.
  FAK: Shoo. Shoo.
PATTY: Shoo. Shoo.
 CONE: Shoo. Shoo.
       (PATTY *screams.*)
PATTY: (*to audience as if drowning*). Help! Help me!
       Help!
 DEAN: Stop . . . (*He walks into their midst.*) . . . What
       goes on here?
PATTY: Eh?
  FAK: Them. . . . One of them.
 CONE: He's alone . . . (*walking up to* DEAN) Nice, isn't
       he?
PATTY: (*they begin to amble round* DEAN). Nice——
  FAK: Cecil Gee——
 CONE: Careful not to crush——
PATTY: Pardon.
  FAK: Excuse me.
 CONE: He don't look very well——
  FAK: Bit daft, ain't he?
PATTY: Hi Mister!

25

FAK: Can you hear?

DEAN: (*amazed*). Hey.

PATTY: He's loose.

FAK: He's loony.

CONE: Quack! Quack!

PATTY: Potty!

FAK: Look!

DEAN: What!

CONE: Mmm . . . pooch!

FAK: Boo!

DEAN: Animals——

CONE: Boo! Boo!

DEAN: —Like stampeding——

PATTY: Bim! Bam!

CONE: Bang! Bang!

FAK: (*bringing out his gun*). Yak! Yak! Yak! Yak!

PATTY: Boo boo boo boo.

CONE: Yak! Yak!

DEAN: Control. Control.

FAK: Yak yak yak yak!

PATTY: Tcha! Tcha! Tcha!

FAK: Yay yak yak yak!

PATTY: Tcha tcha tcha tcha!

DEAN: (*making a great effort to collect himself and dominate them*). What are you trying to do?
    (CONE *behind* DEAN *gives him a sharp blow at the base of the skull—unseen by the others.*)
    Ah!
    (DEAN *collapses forward against* FAK *who is sent staggering away firing his gun wildly.* DEAN *falls and is still.*)

FAK: One o' them! One o' them! One o' them!

CONE: Stop.

FAK: . . . Dead . . . he's dead . . . She'll maim me

26

for this. She'll kill me . . .

CONE: Shut up, slob.

FAK: It ain't you. It ain't you. It's me. It's me she'll
be after. She said not, not for a bit, not after
Aldgate . . . Aldgate . . . Leave it. Come on.
Let's leave it. Someone'll take it away—
perhaps it'll disappear—perhaps it'll melt.
Come on. Let's go. Where'll we go? Let's go to
the flicks. Come on, Patty. Let's go.

CONE: Wake up, stupid.

FAK: (*weeping*). It ain't you. It ain't you.

CONE: O blubber shut up.

FAK: It ain't you. It ain't you.

CONE: Oh— (*dismissing it*). Oh—I'll think of
something.

FAK: What? . . . What? You—you—yes, you will.
That's it, he'll think of something. Yes, you
will, you will, you will, oh well. That's well.
That'll be all right. That'll be all right.

CONE: Yeah. (*Relaxed and drowsy he picks up the gun
and laughs.*)

FAK: What you laughing for?

CONE: He looks a treat.

FAK: A treat . . . A treat . . . a fair treat . . . I feel
good . . . I feel bloody good . . . I feel bloody
wonderful.

PATTY: (*weeping and laughing*). Mucker! . . . Mucker!
. . . Stuck up! . . . That's for you, mucker. You.
You. I hate you!

CONE: There's something about this bloke . . .
something about the way he looks, he don't
look . . . Wonder if he's got a gun.
(CONE *finds some American cigarettes in* DEAN'*s
pocket.*)

27

Yank . . . Is he a yank? . . . Let's get this lot
shifted before someone stumbles over it.

FAK: They got no Yanks.

CONE: Eh?

FAK: They got no Yanks!

CONE: For crying out loud get lifting.

FAK: You'll think of something.

CONE: Yeah.

PATTY: I feel sick.

FAK: Not bad. Not bad eh? . . . Killer! . . . Killer!
. . . Oh! I'm gonna get a whistle sleeker than
this and longer . . . new drains—narrow,
narrow and dark . . . and a new shirt . . . Oh!
White! With French cuffs. And a new tie—and
I'll knot it broad . . . I'm gonna get a
cigarette-holder, thick and stubby. Bamboo
with a gold band.

    I'm gonna get me a great red ruby!
    Rich and bulging and bold like blood.
    Sweet thick pleasure is guttering through me.
    Red! Red! Red! 'll make me feel good.

CHORUS: Killer! Killer! Killer!
    Killer! Killer! Killer!

FAK: Carry it dressy on a thick gold ring;
    Solid and stubby and strong and thick.
    Flash 'em in the looker and stab and sting
    Send them solid and clutch in the mick.

CHORUS: Killer! Killer! Killer!
    Killer! Killer! Killer!

FAK: Sweet old, lovely old, solid gold ruby—
    Deep, sweet, blood warm, sombre and soft.
    Great sweet pleasure is welling all through
      me—
    Loose and easy and warm and free.

28

(*They are in a state of euphoria or post ecstasy,
their minds and nervous system unslung.* STEVE
has helped lull them to this. STEVE *strikes a note.*
DEAN *gets up and considers* CONE, FAK *and*
PATTY.)

DEAN: What is this? What is this? I don't get it . . . I
like to understand things and I don't
understand this . . . It's like some nasty joke
. . . it's like spitting in your eye . . . kind of
nasty and weak and dangerous . . . If I turn
my back on this it'll rot inside me . . . O.K.
fellers, this time you won't get me so fast or so
easy, we'll wait until the moment I choose and
then we'll see who bops who . . .
(DEAN *resumes his corpse posture but chooses a
different part of the stage to lie down. At a sign
from* DEAN, STEVE *strikes a note and wakes the
others.*)

FAK: Ah! Hah!

CONE: Eh? What's up with you?

FAK: (*sheepish*). Oh—sorry.

CONE: What you mean sorry?

FAK: Thought it was them. Thought I heard
something.

CONE: Nit.

FAK: Might've been them, could've been.

CONE: If you'd heard them.

FAK: Yeah, if I'd heard.

CONE: If. Where'd you think Greta's got to?
(*Pause.*)

FAK: Greta'll be along.

CONE: I know she'll be along.
(*Pause.*)

FAK: She'll be along.

29

CONE: She said she'd be here.

FAK: Well . . . (*Pause.*) Here! Where's it gone? Someone's pinched it . . . You've put it somewhere.

PATTY: What's the matter?

FAK: It was here I swear. Oh Gawd!

PATTY: It's there.

FAK: How'd it get there? (*Turning on* CONE.) Very funny, very funny I'm sure. Hah hah.

CONE: Look out! Get that.

(*Enter* DODO. *Apparently about 16 years old with a plain, pale, old face. She might even be an old woman. She wears a man's overcoat too large for her and a big, old hat. She brings on a huge pile of rags, newspapers etc., carrying them, dragging them on a makeshift sledge or pushing them in a pram. She doesn't see the others but she sees the audience and is startled and suspicious. Eventually she decides the best way to get round them is to try and amuse them. She performs any tricks she may know of the simplest, clumsiest kind, making shapes with her fingers resembling animals etc., presently she begins to make noises: clucking, grunting etc., again imitating animals, finally she is at her ease.* PATTY *gets the giggles.*)

PATTY: I wish Maureen could see this.

CONE: Take your tip from me. (*To* DODO) Hiya banana face! What's your name?
(DODO *freezes with fear.*)

DODO: (*inarticulate*). Do . . . do . . . do . . .

CONE: Dodo eh? Hiyah Dodo.

FAK: Hello, Dodo.

CONE: Glad we seen you.

30

PATTY: Ever so glad.

FAK: Ever so glad, eh?

CONE: Because we've got a little present for you.

FAK: A present?

CONE: For her birthday.

FAK: Her birthday?

PATTY: Her birthday.

CONE: A birthday present for her birthday. Let's
show. Let's show her the present.
(CONE *motions them to fetch the "body"*.)

PATTY: Yes! Yes!

FAK: Yeah!

What'd you guess it was, Dodo? What'd you guess?

PATTY: Guess.

FAK: Guess.

CONE: Guess.

PATTY: Guess. Guess.

CONE: Say something, Dodo. Close your eyes and say
what comes into your eyes. Think! Long and
thin——

FAK: Heavy.

CONE: Yeah. Long and thin and heavy . . . eh, Dodo?

PATTY: Yes.

FAK: Long and thin and heavy.

CONE: What is it? What is it, eh?

PATTY: Long and thin and heavy.

FAK: Long and thin and heavy.

CONE: Long and thin and heavy—like a——?

PATTY: It's like a——

FAK: Like a—— (*Touches* DODO).

DODO: Carpet!

FAK: A carpet!

CONE: A carpet! . . . A carpet . . . Who said this girl
was stupid, eh? . . . Who said she was dull . . .

A carpet. My! What a brain. . . . A carpet. . . .
That's right, Dodo. That's absolutely right.
Clever girl. Well done. All right. Show the lady
her carpet. Look, Dodo! Here's your carpet.
Smashing. Persian.

FAK: A carpet.

CONE: Faky-boy. Show the lady her carpet.

FAK: What?

CONE: (*miming*). You take that. And you take that.

PATTY: This, eh?

FAK: What?

PATTY: That! That!

FAK: Oh . . . that?

CONE: Yes, stupid. Patty, you take this.

PATTY: This? This?

FAK: Oh, I see—that!

CONE: When I say "heave": heave. O.K. One! Two!
Three!——

FAK: (*stumbles against* DODO). Oh pardon.

PATTY: Oh!

CONE: Why, you stupid.

FAK: Oh, I'm ever so sorry.

CONE: You stupid clumsy thing, you. Apologize.
Apologize to Dodo.

FAK: Please excuse me. I'm ever so sorry. Beg
pardon.

CONE: A bit more to you——mind the wrinkle.

FAK: The what?

PATTY: The wrinkle! The wrinkle!

FAK: Oh, the wrinkle.

PATTY: If one of you stood in the middle——

CONE: I'll stand in the middle——

FAK: No. I want to.

CONE: No, I want to.

FAK: No, I want to.

CONE: Oh, very well . . .

PATTY: Take your shoes off.

FAK: What!

PATTY: If you think anything of Dodo you'll take your shoes off before you stand on her nice carpet.

FAK: Oh heck.

CONE: Let's all take our shoes off.

FAK: Oh all right. If we all do.
(CONE, FAK *and* PATTY *remove their shoes.*)
Your feet smell.

CONE: They don't.

FAK: They do.

PATTY: You've got a hole in your sock.

FAK: So's he.

PATTY: Cor! Don't it look silly. What a lark. Why don't you mend it?

CONE: Oh, come on. Let's get out of here.

FAK: What about Greta?

CONE: (*irritated*). Let's get out.

FAK: (*to* DODO). Glad you like the present . . . I said glad you like it . . . What you think about the present, eh? . . . You like it, don't you? . . . Well, go on, say something, it's only polite . . . nice, isn't it? . . . I said it's nice . . . it's nice . . . you do like it, don't you? . . . Go on say you do . . . Go on . . . You do like it, don't you . . . you do, don't you . . . You got to say you do . . . you got to. You got to say you do . . . you do, don't you . . . you do—you do, don't you, you do . . . eh? What? . . . What . . . what . . . what . . . what's the matter? I said what's the matter? . . . Oh . . . oh heck . . . oh hell, oh bloody hell . . . oh bloody bloody . . . look!

33

It's going! It's bloody going! I'm bloody taking
it away! Look! Look!

PATTY: What's the matter with him?

FAK: What shall we do with it?

CONE: Wrap it up in brown paper.

FAK: (*seeing* DODO'*s pile of old rags*). They'll do.

DODO: No!

FAK: Eh?

DODO: No!

FAK: What!

DODO: No! No!

(FAK *and* DODO, *their joy growing, tussle for the
rags.*)

DODO: No! No! No! No! No!

FAK: No! No! No! No! No!

PATTY: (*laughing*). Oh silly, silly Faky-boy. Oh my,
isn't it blarney, girl. Oh horrible, horrible.

CONE: My God My God My God My God My God
My God My God.

(FAK *lets go the rags and snatches up the
newspapers.*)

DODO: Oops!

FAK: Yippee!

(*They stand* DEAN *upright and wrap him in
newspapers, winding scotch tape around him to
hold the papers in place. Note:* STEVE *may give
them the tape, if there seems to be a problem
keeping the "body" upright, then* STEVE *may be
able to help with commands on his instruments.*)

DODO: No No No No
Throw Throw Throw Throw
So So So So
Blow Blow Blow Blow
Crow Crow Crow Crow

34

Doe Doe Doe Doe.

CONE: What you got there? Sandwiches?

FAK: Strong and neat. That's what I call a packet.
(*Reading a headline from the paper*) "London
policeman beaten by an iron bar." Hurrah!
(FAK *sticks a hat on* DEAN's *head.*)
Got a penny for the guy, Mister! Got a penny
for the guy.

    Got a penny for the guy.
    Got a penny for the guy.

DODO: Tootle tootle tootle toot.
    Tootle tootle tootle toot.

FAK: Got a penny for the guy.
    Got a penny for the guy.
(STEVE *picks up the rhythm. The rest pretend to
be playing instruments.*)

DODO: Tootle tootle tootle toot.
    Tootle tootle tootle toot.

CONE: Bang Bang Bang Bang.

FAK: Got a penny for the guy.
    Got a penny for the guy.

PATTY: Wow wow wow wow
    Wow wow wow wow.

DODO: Tootle tootle tootle toot.
    Tootle tootle tootle toot.

CONE: Tcha!
(CONE, FAK *and* PATTY *begin to dance round*
DEAN *as round a totem: bellowing words at the
head wrapped in newspaper.*)

PATTY: Wow wow wow wow wow wow wow wow.

FAK: Guy guy guy guy guy guy guy guy.

CONE: Bang bang bang bang bang bang bang bang.
(CONE, FAK *and* PATTY *begin frenziedly to tear
the paper from* DEAN.)

35

CONE: Ah! Ah! Ah! Ah!

FAK: Ah! Ah! Ah! Ah!

PATTY: Ah! Ah! Ah! Ah!

DEAN: Stop.

CONE: (*holding out the American pack*). Cigarette?
(DEAN *stretches out his hand and waits.* CONE *puts the cigarette in* DEAN'*s hand.* CONE *walks away sulking and angry.*)

DEAN: (*including the audience*). We'll now have a little peace—a little tranquillity. I'm serious. I'm calling a truce for one minute. For one whole minute nobody up here is going to do anything and you can all relax. Nothing's going to happen up here. Nothing at all. (*To the others*) You understand?

PATTY &
    FAK: (*in character*). Yes, all right.

DEAN: All right . . . You can just relax. Just let go.
O.K.: one minute from now . . . (*After sufficient time, to* DODO) Feeling better?
(CONE *rises.*)
That's all right. Time's up.
(*For* DODO.)

> Saw a silver feather
> Floating in the sun—
> Reached up and caught it.
> That was one.
>
> Saw a golden nugget
> Glitt'ring down below—
> Dug deep and found it.
> That was two.
>
> Saw a pearly oyster

36

Washed out to sea—
Swam out and fetched it.
That was three.
(CONE *goes as if to exit then, seeing something outside, flattens himself.*)

FAK : (*whispering*). What is it?

CONE : Them.

FAK : Aldgate?

CONE : 'Bout eight of them. All round out there they are.

FAK : Let's have a look.

CONE : Keep back here, you can just—careful! If they see us we won't have a——

FAK : Gawd!

CONE : Where's Greta eh? Where is she? Why ain't she here?

DEAN : Who's out there?

CONE : Never you mind.

DEAN : Friends of yours?

CONE : Yeah, friends of ours. Why don't you go have a little chat.
(*Pause.* DEAN *starts to exit.*)

FAK : They'll smash you.
(*Pause.*)

DEAN : (*to* DODO). Just you wait there, honey. Don't you stir till I come back.

FAK : They'll kill you.
(*Exit* DEAN. CONE, FAK *and* PATTY *watch him outside.*)
Cor!

PATTY : What's happened?

FAK : Cor!

PATTY : Let me see! Let me see!

FAK : Look at that. Will you just look at that.

(FAK *and* PATTY *exit*.)

CONE: What you want to go with him for? Why you
want to go with him? Ain't you going to wait
for Greta? . . . Greta . . . I'll tell her . . . I'll
tell . . . I'll go and find her and tell her . . . tell
Greta . . . Greta . . . Mamma! Mamma! Where
are you, Mamma? Why you left me? . . .
(*Going*) Mamma! (*Off*) Mamma! Greta! . . .
(DODO *plays with the light*. STEVE *starts to tap a
rhythm*. DODO *keeps time allowing the sound and
the texture of the light to govern her body.
Pause*. STEVE *comes to her*.)

STEVE: You're all right. But you let them push you
around such a lot. I mean you let them push
you around such a lot in the play.
(DODO *looks at him, lights start to come up for
interval*. DODO *hastily clears off*.)

(*End of Act One*)

During the interval STEVE *might remain on
stage, attending to his instruments, doing odd
jobs around the stage, chatting to stage hands
etc.*

ACT TWO

STEVE *onstage*.
Blackout.
Enter DEAN, PATTY, FAK *and* DODO *who run about the stage with lighted sparklers weaving patterns in the dark.*

DEAN: Ha ha! Whew! Whew!
PATTY: Whew! Whew!
FAK: Ain't it pretty?
PATTY: Christmas! Christmas!
DODO: (*excited*). Oh—oh.
DEAN: Dodo, here. (*He gives* DODO *a sparkler*.)
DODO: Wheesh! Wheesh! Wheesh!
FAK: Watch!
PATTY: Mine's better.
DEAN: Whew! Whew!
  (*The last sparkler goes out*.)
PATTY: Aren't there any more?
DEAN: I guess not.
PATTY: Oh . . . quiet, isn't it.
FAK: I see you. (*He grabs at* DODO *who laughs and runs away*.)
  (DEAN *laughs*. FAK *laughs uneasily*. FAK *starts to range around the stage*. DEAN, *taking the others, avoids him*.)
  Let's have some light, eh? . . . O.K. . . . O.K. . . . Switch on . . . Kill the black . . . I said kill

the black . . . D'you hear?

DEAN: (*mocking*). D'you hear?

FAK: What?

DEAN: (*mocking*). What.

FAK: What!

PATTY: (*mocking*). What.

FAK: (*roaring*). Ah! Kill the black! Kill the black!
(FAK *lunges violently around the stage.*)

DODO: (*frightened*). Oh . . . Oh . . .

DEAN: Lights! Lights! (*Lighting a match.*) Let's have
the lights.

PATTY: Switch on. Switch on the lights!

DODO: Lights! Lights! Lights!

DEAN: Lights! Lights!
(*Stage Lights on.*)

FAK: (*to* DEAN). Who d'you think you are? Who
d'you think you are, eh? Want to fight? Want
to fight, eh?

DEAN: You're bigger than me.
(FAK *goes roaring at him.* DEAN *leans sideways
and* FAK *blunders in the wall.* PATTY *laughs and
goes over to* DEAN.)

PATTY: Got a fag? . . . Ta.

FAK: (*to* PATTY). Let's go find the fellers.

PATTY: Not for a bit.

FAK: Come on. Come on.

PATTY: Leave me be. I said not for a bit. They'll be
here soon anyway.

DEAN: Where's—what's his name?

PATTY: You mean Cone?

DEAN: The guy who was here.

PATTY: I expect he's put out . . . well, don't you want
to know why?

DEAN: I guess I know why.

40

PATTY: Oo! You are a one. I guess he's gone to tell——
FAK: Shut up.
PATTY: Who are you talking to? (*To* DEAN) How old
      are you? I'm twenty-three.
DEAN: (*smiling*). You don't look twenty-three.
PATTY: O—don't I?
DEAN: You're sixteen.
PATTY: Sixteen! Why—why—I'm twenty-three! I'm
      twenty-three.
      (PATTY's *cigarette has gone out.* DEAN *relights it
      and then without turning his back on* PATTY,
      plays with DODO.)
FAK: Come on, let's go find the fellers.
PATTY: For heaven's sake.
FAK: Why you flapping over him?
PATTY: I'm not flapping.
FAK: Who is he? What's he doing here?
PATTY: O shut up. Take your nose out of my business.
      Buzz off.
      (FAK *starts to go and then comes back.*)
      (*to* DEAN). My favourite colour's true blue, I
      just love true blue—it's just *the* colour. I've got
      lots and lots—this is true blue.
DEAN: Yes, I saw it was blue.
PATTY: You're subtle. Oh! I've got lots of true blue—
      lots and lots. I've even got true blue——
DEAN: What?
PATTY: Nothing.
DEAN: (*smiling*). What were you going to say?
PATTY: Oh, nothing, nothing. What do you like to eat?
DEAN: Oh . . .
PATTY: I think American food, it's—ooh just lovely.
DEAN: You like American food?
PATTY: I've seen it in magazines,

41

DEAN: And Cone's gone to tell who?

FAK: Don't say.

PATTY: Greta.

DEAN: Greta, eh.

PATTY: You needn't bother about her.

FAK: Why! Why needn't he? He'd bloody well better!

PATTY: What do you like to drink?

DEAN: Oh—what do you like?

PATTY: Bourbon.

DEAN: Bourbon!

PATTY: Bourbon on the rocks.

DEAN: My.

FAK: Wipe the grin off your face.

DEAN: Was I smiling?

PATTY: Who asked you to butt in? I thought you'd gone.

FAK: Well I was but then I thought I wouldn't. Do you want to?

PATTY: Not likely. I ain't going west with everything going pop pop and the law and everyone thinking they're General Montgomery.

FAK: Any other time, you'd jump at it.

PATTY: Oh leave me be.

(DEAN, *playing with* DODO, *blows his fingers down one by one.*)

DEAN: Where've they gone? . . . Now where have they gone? . . . Eh! Now you . . . Dear oh dear . . . where can they be?

(PATTY *brings out her home perm outfit.*)

PATTY: I just never will understand this.

DEAN: What have you got there? Why it's a home perm.

PATTY: Do you know about them?

DEAN: Do I know about them? How many times have

I watched my sister! Gee! This takes me back.

FAK: What's that for?

DEAN: It's the wave lotion. You curl the hair up in these—see? And damp it with the wave lotion . . . and this is the rinse: You put it on to stop the wave lotion working. You have to be careful with this stuff. Don't use any metal with it and don't get it in your eyes or anything.

PATTY: It's awful, isn't it?

DEAN: No, it isn't, it's simple really—when you know . . . tell you what: I'll help you.

PATTY: O . . . O . . . well thanks—but . . . er . . .

DEAN: Why I'd love to.

FAK: I saw you at the Aldgate bash!

DEAN: Eh?

FAK: 'Swear I saw him there.

PATTY: What are you getting at?

FAK: You was there, wasn't you?

DEAN: No . . . what was the Aldgate bash?

FAK: Go on! Don't you read the papers?
(DEAN *shrugs his shoulders.*)
You missed something. There was a lovely photo of some of our lot after that.

PATTY: Stupid, getting their faces about.

FAK: Bottles and razors all down the Commercial road just as the flicks were coming out. And a lonely copper clapped in his daisy. Cor! You should've seen him. One eye hanging out and his nose all over the side of his face, he wasn't half slammed. Coo! They hung it on him—and funny thing—you had to laugh: he said he was getting married next day.

PATTY: (*excited*). Oh . . . Oh . . .

FAK: Take you some time.

PATTY : They're always after the Aldgate lot.

FAK : Yeah. They're our regulars.

DEAN : Do they come and fight you back?

FAK : We get plenty of warning.

PATTY : They daren't.

FAK : Yeah. That was a real good do—some of their chaps'll never walk straight again . . . one of our lot lost a finger.

DEAN : (*sickened*). Oh.
(*Long pause.*)

PATTY : Aren't you bored? I'm bored.

FAK : We could go to the flicks.

PATTY : What's on?

FAK : Anybody got a paper?
(DODO *holds out one of hers.*)

DEAN : Sixth of March.

FAK : Ava Gardner. (*Or other, Author's note*) At the Dominion—I think. . . . Let's get a guy and go collecting . . . money in it.

DEAN : Where'd you get a guy?

PATTY : (*catty*). Dodo'd do.

DEAN : Let's perm Patty!

PATTY : What!

DEAN : Let's perm you, Patty. Where's Patty's perm?

PATTY : Go on, it'd look ever so silly.

DEAN : (*charming her*). Monsieur Dean! Coiffeur des dames.

PATTY : Well—so long as you're sure it'll be all right.

DEAN : Yippee! Catch! Curlers? Mug?

STEVE : I'll get you a mug. (*He exits and returns with a mug.*)

DEAN : Lotion? Thanks.

PATTY : It's here.

DEAN : Cast it in . . . anybody got a comb?

44

FAK: Yes.

PATTY: Is it clean?

DEAN: Of course it's clean—no. Mine's cleaner.

PATTY: Thanks, we'll use mine.

DEAN: Cotton wool?

FAK: There's some here.

DEAN: O.K. Fak! Seat for the lady. Dodo, you hold this paper and read. Can you read? Atta girl! Fak: mug and cotton. Patty: papers and curlers. All ready? Good. Now, get this:

DODO: Divide . . .

DEAN: Divide?

DODO: Divide scalp into three sections: from ear to ear and down centre back. See fig. 4.

PATTY: Be careful.

DEAN: Scalp in three sections from ear to ear and down centre back. O.K.?

FAK: O.K.

DODO: Take a section the size of a curler.

DEAN: Curler.

PATTY: Curler.

DODO: Thoroughly saturate with the lotion.

DEAN: Lotion.

FAK: Lotion.

DODO: Fold an end paper over and under.

DEAN: End paper.

PATTY: One of these?

DEAN: Yip! Like this, see?

FAK: That?

DEAN: Ya.

PATTY: Just a minute——

DEAN: Faster there——

DODO: Wind it firmly to the root of the hair.

DEAN: Wind it firmly to the root of the hair. Patty,

45

you're going to look lovely.

PATTY: I hope so I'm sure.

DEAN: O.K. More. More.

PATTY: Mind you do it proper.

DEAN: Leave it to us. Now: let's have a system.

PATTY: Take a section the size of a curler.

DEAN: Take a section the size of a curler.

PATTY: Thoroughly saturate with the lotion.

FAK: Thoroughly saturate with the lotion.

PATTY: Fold an end paper over and under.

DODO: Fold an end paper over and under.

PATTY: Wind it firmly to the root of the hair.

DEAN: Wind it firmly to the root of the hair . . .
Again!

PATTY: Take a section the size of a curler.

DEAN:
DODO: } Take a section the size of a curler.
FAK:

PATTY: Thoroughly saturate with the lotion.

DEAN:
DODO: } Thoroughly saturate with the lotion.
FAK:

PATTY: Fold an end paper over and under.

DEAN:
DODO: } Fold an end paper over and under.
FAK:

PATTY: Wind it firmly to the root of the hair.

DEAN:
DODO: } Wind it firmly to the root of the hair.
FAK:

DEAN: ⌉ Take a section the size of a curler
DODO: | Thoroughly saturate with the lotion
PATTY: ⌈ Fold an end paper over and under
& FAK: ⌋ Wind it firmly to the root of the hair.

46

DEAN: Again!

DEAN: ⎱ Take a section the size of a curler
DODO: ⎰ Thoroughly saturate with the lotion
PATTY: ⎱ Fold an end paper over and under
& FAK: ⎰ Wind it firmly to the root of the hair.

    Take a section
    Saturate
    Fold a paper
    Wind it firm.

DEAN: When the curls are fully *wound*.

PATTY: ⎫
DODO: ⎬ Section.
& FAK: ⎭

DEAN: Sit fifteen minutes out of *draughts*.

PATTY: ⎫
DODO: ⎬ Saturate.
& FAK: ⎭

DEAN: After that take out a *test* curl.

PATTY: ⎫
DODO: ⎬ Paper.
& FAK: ⎭

DEAN: See the curl is strong and well *formed*.

PATTY: ⎫
DODO: ⎬ Wind.
& FAK: ⎭

DEAN: If the test wave's weak and *poor*.

PATTY: ⎫
DODO: ⎬ Sec.
& FAK: ⎭

DEAN: Take a look at figure five. (My! It is poor).

PATTY: ⎫
DODO: ⎬ Sat.
& FAK: ⎭

DEAN: Curl the curl again and *leave*.

47

PATTY:
DODO: } Pap.
& FAK:

DEAN: A few more minutes, then unwind.

DEAN: } Careful not to sit in draughts.
FAK: Sec.
DODO: Sat.
PATTY: Pap.
FAK: Wind.

FAK: Use no metal with the lotion.
DODO: Sec.
PATTY: Sat.
DEAN: Pap.
DODO: Wind.

DODO: } May be set in many styles (See note attached).
PATTY: Sec.
DEAN: Sat.
FAK: Pap.
PATTY: Wind.

     (The scene, while remaining light-hearted,
     becomes riotous.)

DODO: Saturate. Saturate. Saturate. Saturate.

DEAN: } Sec sat pap wind!
PATTY: } Sec sat pap wind!
& FAK:

DODO: Lots of lotion lots of lotion!

PATTY: } Sec sat pap wind!
& FAK: } Sec sat pap wind!

DEAN: Pour the rinse in! Pour the rinse in!

DEAN: } Pour the rinse in! Pour the rinse in!
PATTY: } Sec! Sat! Sick! Sock! Pip! Pap!
& FAK: } Pop! Pup! Pep! Pump! Pimp! Pamp! Wind!

48

(*Enter* CONE. DODO *pours the rinse into the mug of lotion.*)

PATTY: She's put the rinse in the lotion.

DEAN: (*laughing*). Ah—! Oh dear! Oh dear me! Oh dear me! Oh dear! Oh—you shouldn't have done that. Oh dear . . . What's it say here? After fifteen minutes rinse . . . Oh dear . . .

FAK: Smells terrible.

PATTY: It's gone green.

FAK: Let's pour it on and see what happens.

PATTY: What!

DEAN: She'd go bald. How'd you like a wig, Patty?

PATTY: Thanks very much.

DEAN: Fak'll spit on you.

FAK: Looks like it'd melt sixpence.

DODO: Let's try.

PATTY: Don't waste sixpence.

DEAN: You could blind somebody with this.

CHORUS: That's an idea.

(CONE *laughs gently.*)

PATTY: Go on. Laugh. Have a good giggle. Very funny I'm sure. What about me? What about me? I'm laughing myself silly. Look at me. Look! I'll look wonderful won't I? A real treat. You make me sick. Look at it. Look at it. It's all mucked up. Ugh! It's horrible.

(DODO *tries to help her.*)

Ugh! Get away. Don't touch me you nasty little thing. Leave me be. Leave me be.

DEAN: Oh, Patty, you can wash it.

CHORUS: Wash! Wash! It's chemical and it needs chemical to get it off—and the chemical's there—ruined. All it's good for is blinding people. Oh, you're so stupid. I wish I'd never set eyes on you. . . .

49

I wish I was at home all nice and quiet in bed.

DEAN: Oh, Pat, it was a lot of fun, wasn't it?

PATTY: Very funny for you, I'm sure.

DEAN: Tell you what! I'll buy you a new perm. Come on, let's go and get it washed, eh?

(DEAN *sees* CONE *move as if to stop him leaving. Exit* PATTY. *Pause. Re-enter* PATTY.)

PATTY: There's something out there—big and funny—I felt it go past me in the dark.

CONE: Let's dress up as guys and go collecting.

FAK: What?

CONE: Let's dress up as guys.

FAK: What for?

CHORUS: Let's dress up.

FAK: Cor break my bleeding heart! We got to dress up? (*To* PATTY.) What you shivering for?

PATTY: It's Greta. It's Greta.

FAK: What you mean it's Greta?

PATTY: It's Greta, there's something funny going on.

FAK: Something funny?

PATTY: It's Greta.

CONE: (*to* DEAN). What you say, Yank?
(*Pause.*)

DEAN: Very well.

FAK: Oh well, what junk for me. What dress? There's not enough here for five.

PATTY: There is.

FAK: How many are there? One, two, three, four, five. There's not enough for five people.

PATTY: 'Course there's enough for five—Dodo's dressed up anyway.

(*They start to cover themselves from head to foot with the old coats and blankets, masking their faces and covering their heads.*)

50

CONE: Please to remember
ALL: Please to remember
Please to remember
Please to remember the fifth of November.

Please to remember
Please to remember
Please to remember the fifth of November.
(*Enter* GRETA *dressed as the others. She mingles
with them unnoticed.*)
Please to remember
Please to remember
Please to remember the fifth of November
Please to remember the fifth of November
Gunpowder, treason and plot.
(*All six are strung out across the stage.*)
DODO: (*in terror, her hat falling off*). There are six . . .
there are six . . . Oh! . . . Oh! . . . Oh!
DEAN: All right honey, it's me, Dean, I'm here.
(DEAN *goes to* DODO, *the others reform so that
their identity is confused.* DEAN *is at first
guarded, then as he gets more confident, almost
contemptuous; but after he fails to unmask*
GRETA *he loses his psychological balance and the
others can get at him.*)
CONE: Dean.
DEAN: Yes?
CONE: That your name, Dean?
DEAN: Yeah.
FAK: Dean.
PATTY: Dean.
CONE: Where you from, Dean?
DEAN: The U.S.
PATTY: What part of the U.S.?

51

DEAN: New York.

PATTY: (*impressed*). New York!

FAK: Do you know Pampinato?

DEAN: Pampinato? Who's he.

CONE: Where d'you live in New York, Dean?

DEAN: Where do I live!

FAK: Where d'you live?

DEAN: I have an apartment.

CONE: An apartment.

PATTY: An apartment.

DEAN: I share an apartment.

CONE: Share.

PATTY: Share.

DEAN: This is very stupid, very stupid. Cone, for heaven's sake, take off that silly mask.

GRETA: (*speaking with an Australian accent*). Who d'you share your apartment with, Dean?

DEAN: Uh?

(*As he turns to the unfamiliar voice* CONE *moves across his vision.* PATTY *speaks behind him,* GRETA *changes her position.*)

PATTY: Who d'you share with?

DEAN: A friend.

CONE: Who? . . . What's his name?

PATTY: Afraid?

FAK: Afraid to get mixed up?

DEAN: This is stupid! Stupid!

FAK: You're trying to put us off.

PATTY: You're afraid to tell us.

CONE: Is there any harm in telling us?

DEAN: Of course there's no harm.

PATTY: Then why not tell us?

DEAN: This is a stupid situation.

CONE: Is this a stupid situation?

52

FAK: You know Petticoat Lane?

DEAN: What else?

FAK: Nice district Aldgate.

DEAN: I wouldn't know.

FAK: Petticoat Lane is in Aldgate.

DEAN: Why don't you go play Guy Fawkes?

CONE: Who shares your apartment?

DEAN: Conrad.

PATTY: Con——

FAK: Con——

CONE: Conrad who?

DEAN: Scaeffer.

CONE: Conrad Scaeffer.

PATTY: Who else do you know?

CONE: Who else are your friends?

PATTY: Have you any friends?

DEAN: Have I any friends?

FAK: Who else?

CONE: Name them.

DEAN: Clive West, Mary Allen, Zachary Hope,
        Alma——

CONE: Why not give the real names?

PATTY: The real names.

FAK: The people you really go around with.

DEAN: This is idiotic, fantastic.

FAK: Gringo!

GRETA: Pivesky!

FAK: Turps!

CONE: Pampinato!

DEAN: I don't know them.

PATTY: Why should you know them?

CONE: What reason have you to know them?

FAK: Did we say you did?

(By an effort of concentration, and by identifying

53

the voices, DEAN *has eliminated* PATTY, FAK *and*
CONE, *now he tries to get hold of* GRETA.)

DEAN: You! You! Who——?

(GRETA *has slipped away,* DEAN *finds* CONE.)

CONE: Who's Scaeffer?

DEAN: Journalist?

PATTY: What paper?

DEAN: I—I——

PATTY: Showgirl—Mary Allen?

DEAN: No—a——

GRETA: What?

DEAN: Stenographer.

PATTY: Who for?

DEAN: Men in shoes—in a shoe company.

CONE: Name?

DEAN: How should I know? I don't——

FAK: Pampinato.

DEAN: What?

CONE: Know that name?

DEAN: I—I heard it.

CONE: So you heard it!

GRETA: Your mother was born in——?

DEAN: Sure—I mean Detroit.

GRETA: Sure?

DEAN: Sure I'm sure.

CONE: Absolutely sure?

DEAN: Why not! Why not!

PATTY: Brothers!

DEAN: Brothers!

FAK: Brothers.

CONE: Brothers.

DEAN: Brothers, brothers my mother was born in . . .

CONE: Pampinato!

DEAN: Yes?

54

CONE: You seen him.

DEAN: I——

PATTY: Your friends——

FAK: They'll get you into trouble.

PATTY: Catch me out. Catch! Catch!

DEAN: No.

GRETA: Who's Mary Pivesky?

CONE: You know her.

PATTY: Gringo.

DEAN: Who? Who?

FAK: Don't know him?

DEAN: Not said——

CONE: The shoemaker——

DEAN: What?

PATTY: You deny——

DEAN: Shoe? Shoe?

PATTY: Said you——

FAK: —Get it out——

PATTY: Say you——

DEAN: No shoe——

PATTY: Said——

FAK: Get——

CONE: Get——

GRETA: Mother born Pittsburgh.

DEAN: Mamma!

> (*Climax.* DEAN *would be finished but* GRETA *has lost interest and moves away, possibly to talk to* STEVE, *the focus of action seems to go with her.*)

CONE: Lepstein.

FAK: You know him.

CONE: He's a friend of yours.

PATTY: Say Gringo.

CONE: Know him?

FAK: Shoemaker.

55

PATTY: Liar.

CONE: You're lying.

FAK: Who's—Who's——

CONE: Who's Zachary Hope?

PATTY: You won't tell us.

FAK: You're afraid.

CONE: You're afraid.

FAK: What are you afraid of?

PATTY: Afraid.

CONE: Afraid to tell.

FAK: Tell us.

PATTY: Tell.

CONE: Stop . . . Notice something?
(*Pause.*)

FAK: No one's talking.

CONE: That's right . . . No one's talking . . . Why you not talking, Dean? . . . You know? . . . he thinks we're stupid.

FAK: Stupid?

CONE: Look at his face. Look at his face. We make him sick. "Take off that silly mask, Cone, you make me sick."

FAK: Make him talk!

PATTY: Talk!

CONE: Where's Dodo? Where's the little bitch? Come here! Come here! Gotcha! All right Dodo: tell Dean to talk. Tell your friend to speak.

DODO: Speak.

CONE: Louder Dodo, louder.

DODO: Speak. Speak.
(DEAN *lunges at* CONE *who instinctively gives way*, DEAN *seizes* DODO *and holds her*.)

CONE: (*screaming*). Answer. Answer. Answer.

FAK: Sock.

56

PATTY: Smash.

CONE: Why won't you answer?

DEAN: Because I won't submit to this degradation.

FAK: Eh?

CONE: Degradation!

PATTY: (*losing control, a howl from the depths*).
Yawooerl.

CONE: Yoweeoch. Yoweeoch.

PATTY: Yawooerl. Yawooerl. Ugh! Ugh!

FAK: Whaow. Aherooigh. Aherooigh.

> (*Screaming with anger and frustration* PATTY,
> FAK *and* CONE *fall upon* DEAN. FAK *raises his gun
> to club* DEAN. GRETA, *a schoolmaster's cane in
> her hand, strikes something sharply.*)

GRETA: Stop.

FAK: Eh?

GRETA: (*quietly*). Drop it.

> (FAK *drops the gun.* GRETA *gently knocks* FAK,
> CONE *and* PATTY *aside. As she approaches* DEAN
> *he takes up the mug of rinse. She stretches out
> her hand and waits.* DEAN *puts it into her hand,
> she drinks and smashes the mug.*)

DEAN: My.

> (GRETA *divests herself of part of her disguise.
> Her hair is long, straight and red, falling from
> her brow like a Japanese lion wig. Her face is
> very heavily made up and almost dead white. She
> catches up the corner of the blanket she is
> wearing and loops it over her arm to give herself
> a swashbuckling air.*)

My.

> (CONE *goes to* GRETA *and plays following scene
> touching her hair, her hand, her arm.*)

GRETA: (*lazily*). What's been doing, eh? Up? Cooking?

Where did the gun come from?

CONE: Fak.

(*An atmosphere of threat emanates from* GRETA. *Pause.*)

FAK: Well, I give it you. (*He is very frightened.*) I was going to give it you. (*Pause.*) I was.

CONE: Got it off his old man.

(*Pause.*)

GRETA (*waving* FAK *away with the cane*). No guns.

(FAK *very depressed retires well out of reach.*)

(*to* CONE). Mind my hair.

CONE: (*privileged*). Sorry.

GRETA: You're a drag.

CONE: (*knowing she doesn't mean it*). And what else?

GRETA: What's that?

CONE: Fireworks.

GRETA: You're kidding me.

CONE: Yes they are.

GRETA: Well well, what'll you lot get up to next? Fireworks. Well, I s'pose even he (FAK) is safe with a sparkler. Hey, move over.

CONE: No you.

GRETA: (*good humoured*). No you. Go on, move over.

CONE: Oh!

GRETA: Well, I told you. What else has been happening?

CONE: He turned up.

GRETA: Oh yes, him. (*She heaves herself round to stare at* DEAN *who stares back. After a while she turns away but remains very conscious of him.*) Mm . . . Well what else have you been up to? Come on tell me, tell me about the fireworks.

CONE: Fak found 'em, he knocked them off a lorry.

GRETA: Fak's had a busy day Fak has.

CONE : Was standing outside a caff not far from
Hendon Central, driver'd gone in for a cuppa,
and we just happened to be there having a
chat, and I saw the lorry didn't have no driver.
O.K. I says to Fak, now your chance, and so
while I keeps a look out—you know the way I
can so no one notices—he heaved himself up
over the side in no time and then what do you
think . . . well?

GRETA : (*her mind on* DEAN) Mm?

CONE : Oh.
(*Long pause.* GRETA *laughs gently.* CONE *goes
round the stage banging and breaking things.*
GRETA *takes no notice.*)

CONE : What about me? What about me?

GRETA : What about you? This about you.
(GRETA *beats* CONE *up in an easy, lazy, rather
splendid manner. He gives himself up in a sort of
ecstasy. When she has done he lies relaxed and
peaceful.*)

DEAN : (*sickened*). North. South. East. West. Foot
kicks face and mouth bites belly. Kiss me Jock,
that's right.

GRETA : Eh? . . . Oh are you still here?

DEAN : My God.

GRETA : Where did you say your mother came from?
(*Before* DEAN *can answer she has turned her
attention to the others.*)

GRETA : (*cheerily*). What a lot! What a mess! What a
look out eh? Right! Wake up! Look lively!
Jump to it! Show a leg there! Right! When I
come into the room stand up! Good morning.

PATTY
& FAK : Eh? What?

CONE: Morning! Morning!

PATTY
& FAK: Morning Miss.

GRETA: Good morning. Stand up! Right! Sit down!

CONE: Please Miss I've got a pain in my leg.

GRETA: (*beating him*). No excuses.

CONE: Yaooer! Yaooer!

FAK: Please Miss, here's an apple.

GRETA: Thanks boy, back to your place. (*To audience*) Wake up! Wake up! Right! Maps! Blackboard! Chalk!

FAK: Please Miss may I be excused?

GRETA: No, stay behind and fill up the inkwells. If a herring and a half cost four farthings?

PATTY: Sevenpence please Miss.

GRETA: Right! Come to the top. (*To audience*) Pay attention! I shall get to you in a minute. Right! In fourteen hundred and ninety-two——

DEAN: (*almost unconsciously automatic reply*). Columbus sailed the ocean blue.

GRETA: Wrong. King Alfred burnt the cakes. (*To* FAK) Spell Miscellaneous.

PATTY: M—I—S—S—er . . . er . . .

GRETA: Right! Right! Right! Write it on the blackboard. (*To* FAK) Hey! What's that?

FAK: Please Miss, nothing Miss, it's a note, Miss.

GRETA: Let me see. Oo! You wicked boy, go wash your hands this instant.
(PATTY, FAK *and* CONE *have gone wild, laughing, playing, somersaulting, etc.*)

GRETA: (*to audience*). Right, you! Two and three-quarters from five and five-eighths? Kings and Queens of England from George the first *backwards*? Battle of Botany Bay? Wrong!

60

Wrong! Wrong!
(GRETA *is madly waving her cane around and now gets it in her eye. She roars and bellows with pain, clutching her eye.*)

DEAN: What is it? What's wrong? Can I help? Please let me—let me have a look. Is it bad?
(GRETA *now blubbering in a hurt and shaken fashion allows him to look at her eye. But once he's doing it he finds himself looking into an eye that's looking right back at him. She begins to rumble with amusement.* DEAN *draws back, not knowing whether she was teasing him. The others laugh with her. Presently the laughter subsides. Pause.*)

GRETA: What you doing sailor boy?
What you doing sailor love?
What you doing ship ahoy?
What you doing little dove?

What you doing little monkey?
What you doing little donkey?
What you doing little fancy?
What you doing little love?
(*Pause. Her feeling of good humour is reflected by* FAK, CONE *and* PATTY. *Suddenly but subtly* GRETA's *feeling changes, she is listening.* CONE *too starts to listen.*)

FAK: What is it? What's the matter?

CONE: Ssh.
(*Pause.*)

GRETA: (*not very excited*). Hear it?

CONE: (*rather tense*). Yeah.
(CONE *goes and looks out.*)

GRETA: Well?

61

CONE: I don't know.
    (*He goes again, this time right off. Pause.*)
FAK: Yeah, now I can hear it.
PATTY: What is it eh?
FAK: Listen.
PATTY: I can't hear nothing . . . we going to find our lot eh? Our fellers?
FAK: Dunno.
PATTY: Eh? Eh?
FAK: I dunno.
    (*Pause. Re-enter* CONE.)
CONE: There's something on.
GRETA: What d'you mean?
CONE: I don't know.
GRETA: (*languid*). Well——
CONE: Shall I get the others?
GRETA: Well—
    (*Pause.*)
CONE: I don't like it, let's get the others.
GRETA: O.K., why not?
CONE: You coming?
GRETA: Me?
CONE: Yes.
GRETA: I don't think I'll come.
CONE: Why? Why not?
GRETA: Don't think I'll come, think I'll have a bit of a nap.
CONE: A nap.
GRETA: Yeah a bit of a sleep. (*To* FAK) You going. Not her.
PATTY: I want to. I want to.
GRETA: Harrow Road, yes? You first.
    (*She listens then motions* FAK *and* PATTY *to go. Exit* FAK *and* PATTY.)

62

CONE: Where'll you nap?

GRETA: Oh . . . here . . . ain't you going?

CONE: He's not for you . . . not for you . . . is he?

GRETA: See you later . . . see you here.

CONE: Is he?

GRETA: Oh get off.

(*Pause. Exit* CONE. GRETA *turns slowly and sleepily, is seen to be pregnant. Sees* DEAN *watching her.*)

Oh yes, you. . . . Mm . . .

(*She rises and exits slowly.*)

DEAN: What's going on here?

STEVE: Search me.

(*The lights fade, house lights coming up. Exit* DEAN, STEVE *and* DODO.)

(*End of Act Two*)

ACT THREE

An hour or so later.
Dark stage.
STEVE *playing a terrible noise.*

DEAN: (*off*). Dodo! Dodo! Dodo!
    (*Noise. Enter* CONE.)
CONE: (*to* STEVE). Where's Greta?
STEVE: Don't know.
CONE: Fight! Fight! It's a fight! Out! Out! Out!
    There! Got it? A gang fight! Pampinato!
    Aldgate! Bang! Bang! (*To the audience*)
    Crackle! Crackle! Behind you! Behind you!
    Behind your head! Turn your head—what's
    behind? What? What?—As you turn your
    head—on your neck! Neck! Feel it! Too dark
    to see but there's something behind—feel it!
    Can you smell something. Can you? Can you
    smell it? Breath! What is it? What you
    breathing, breathing in, in, into yourself? Can
    you breathe? Can you? Can you breathe? Ah!
    Ah! You can't! You can't breathe! You can't!
    Ah! Ah!
    (*Enter* PATTY *running,* CONE *catches her by her*
    coat and swings her round and round, letting her
    go and catching her again.)
PATTY: (*screaming*). Ah! Ah! Ah!

64

CONE: (*laughing*). Ha, ha. Done! Done! Hah hah.
(CONE *lets go her coat and is himself flung
offstage by the momentum. Silence. Pause.*)
PATTY: (*screaming almost soundlessly*). Fak! Fak! Fak!
Fak!
(*Pause. Enter* DODO *blind and blundering, she
bumps into* PATTY *and clutches her.*)
PATTY: (*a screaming whisper*). No! No! Ugh! Go away!
Agh! Agh!
(DODO *clings to* PATTY *who tries to scrape her
off, both consumed with terror and hysteria.*)
DODO: Oh—oh—oh——
PATTY: No! Don't touch me! Agh! Agh!
(*This encounter goes on for a while and against
it rises a drumming sequence, or sequence of
intense, rhythmical, complicated noise. Finally*
PATTY *exits and* DODO *crawls under some rags,
but the noise continues.*)
DEAN: (*off*). Dodo! Dodo! Where are you? Dodo!
(*Enter* DEAN.)
Dodo! Dodo!
(DODO *burrows deeper under the rags, the
movement catches* DEAN's *eye.*)
Dodo . . . Look! I've got something for you . . .
Look Dodo, look it's me, you're all right with
me . . . it's me, don't be afraid, don't be afraid
Dodo . . . I'm strong and I understand . . . it's
terrible, terrible to be weak to try and bear the
terror pressing in on your imagination . . . each
moment as it passes is a moment won from
fear of being hurt . . . but what if they should
come tonight? What if they should get you
tonight? Or tomorrow . . . or next week . . .
and when the moment comes . . . when they

get you . . . oh Dodo! I understand, I understand your fear. There's no loving trust that I withhold from you. Every privilege of my strength I share with you. There, there. (*Pause.*)

STEVE: What's happened to your hand?

DEAN: Oh, I don't know, it got burnt, something burnt it out there. I don't know.
(STEVE *gets something to treat the hand.*)
There. There, that's all right. I'm here, nothing can happen now. They can't hurt you now.
(STEVE *returns and starts dressing the hand.*)

DEAN: This makes me so angry, so angry—all this.
(*Enter* CONE.)

CONE: (*to* DEAN). Where is she?

DEAN: Who?

CONE: Where? Where is she?

DEAN: Greta?

CONE: Where is she?

DEAN: How should I know? What do you want with her? She can look after herself I guess.

CONE: (*to* STEVE). You seen her?

STEVE: No.

DEAN: My God, this mess, this waste, this viciousness.

STEVE: Why be angry?

DEAN: Why be angry? Why be angry? It concerns me! It concerns me! I'm part of the human race and this waste—this violence—this degradation—it betrays humanity, it betrays mankind. That's why I'm angry. Thanks, I can manage by myself. If people will only have patience and intelligence and will power there's nothing we can't master and control. All this mess, this filth—and it's not us who suffer, not us, not

66

the strong ones—people like that woman, they
don't suffer—no, it's this child. What a
responsibility they have, people like her: self-
respect, self-discipline, love, decency, mutual
trust, all gone, the things weaker people can
build their lives on, live in peace and security.
Mutual social laws, the bedrock you can build
your happiness on. And it's our responsibility:
people like you and me and her. In all humility
we have to carry the world, we have to educate
and love—but when I think of that woman:
loose, vicious, destructive——

CONE: Hey! . . . You!

DEAN: Yes?

CONE: After I left . . .

DEAN: Well?

CONE: You know when I mean——

DEAN: I'm afraid I don't.

CONE: You know when I mean—after I left—here—a
bit ago—you were left with her—alone—Well,
what happened?

DEAN: What do you mean what happened?

CONE: What did you do?

DEAN: What did we do?

CONE: What did you do together?

DEAN: Nothing.

CONE: Nothing?

DEAN: No.

CONE: Go on! . . . Go tell us another. That's right.
Thousands'd believe you.

DEAN: I'm telling you the truth.

CONE: Rubbish. (*Pause.*) What's the time?

DEAN: You've got a watch.

CONE: Yeah but it's stopped.

67

DEAN: Why not put it right?

STEVE: One ten.

CONE: Oh well, she won't be long then will she?
(*Enter* FAK.)
Seen her?

FAK: Ain't she here?

CONE: No.

FAK: She'll be about.

CONE: Go and look for her. Go back the Regal, down
the green.

FAK: What me?

CONE: Yes.

FAK: Why don't you go?

CONE: Said I'd see her here.

FAK: I'm tired.

CONE: Said I'd see her.

FAK: You go, I'll wait. Cor there's a bimp out there
—millions, well hundreds, thought I saw
Pampinato, that give me a turn.

DEAN: Who's out there?

FAK: Who's out there!

DEAN: Aldgate?

FAK: Who else?

CONE: Where's Patty?

FAK: ... Oh Gawd ... I lost her ... I lost Patty
... Where she got to? Forgot all about her I
did till you mentioned ... Where's Patty? got
excited with the bashing and ... forgot her ...

CONE: Go and look for her.

FAK: Yeah, yeah. I better hadn't I?

CONE: Back of the Regal, down the green.

FAK: Think she'll be there?

CONE: She'll be there—and if you see Greta——

FAK: Yeah?

CONE: Bring her back here.

FAK: See me bring her back!

CONE: Well, tell her! Tell her!

FAK: Yeah, O.K. O.K.

(*Exit* FAK. *Pause.*)

DEAN: (*to* DODO). How you feeling eh? Better? Ready to face the world? No, no, don't hide your head . . . don't hide. You've got to face fear Dodo, you've got to face evil, otherwise it gets bigger and bigger, not looking at it, pretending it's not there—if you run away from evil—no you've got to fight it back, and you've got to make yourself strong, strong and clever, stupidity is a sin, a sin Dodo, because if you're stupid you can't see the evil in the world, and you can't fight it effectively . . . Oh Dodo, am I asking too much? Nothing, then, nothing, you just lean on me.

(*Pause.*)

CONE: You swear nothing happened?

DEAN: Yes.

(*Pause.*)

CONE: (*to* STEVE). Got any dice?

STEVE: Dice? Can get you some.

CONE: O.K.

(STEVE *exits. Pause. Re-enters with dice which* CONE *takes and starts throwing, getting more violent.*)

DEAN: Must you make such a racket?

CONE: What?

DEAN: You're making a lot of noise.

CONE: Why not? Why shouldn't I?

DEAN: This child's asleep.

CONE: So bloody what?

69

DEAN: Stop that!

CONE: Shut your cakehole.

DEAN: Stop that.

CONE: Get knotted.

(DEAN *rises.* CONE *picks up a weapon, likewise* DEAN. *They face each other across the stage.*)

CONE: Don't you come near me . . . I know your kind, judo—toss you a mile . . . If you come near me I'll bash you.

(*Pause.* DODO *blubbering quietly.*)

What you doing here? Who are you?

DEAN: Don't frighten the child.

CONE: Like hell I won't—Why you hanging round eh?

DEAN: We've been through that.

CONE: And got nowhere.

DEAN: You tried hard enough.

CONE: Get back—Look, stop talking, stop going on. I don't give—look, just get out, go away, go away, go away and get lost. Before she comes back.

DEAN: That woman?

CONE: Don't ask any questions, don't talk, just go, get out, go.

DEAN: Like hell I will.

(*Pause.*)

CONE: What happened after I'd gone?

DEAN: I told you.

CONE: What happened?

DEAN: I'm not telling you again.

(*Pause.*)

CONE: Maybe it's all right then eh? Maybe it's all right?

DEAN: So little self-respect. So little self-control.

(*Enter* FAK *panting and carrying* PATTY.)

What's the matter? What's happened?

FAK: Found her, she'd fainted, up by Church Street she was.

CONE: Seen Greta?

FAK: Who? No. What'll we do eh? What'll we do?

DEAN: Where's Steve? Steve!

STEVE: Eh?

FAK: Don't shout. It's crawling with them outside— millions of them—well, lots. Had an 'orrible time coming back, bent double I was most the way—cor she's a fair weight, she don't look it but my she's heavy.

(PATTY *beginning to come round.* CONE *starts to throw dice, gently, but unhappily.*)

PATTY: Oh . . . oh . . . oh . . .

DEAN: There, that's all right, you're all right now.

FAK: We're here.

PATTY: Oh . . . oh I want to hide, I want to disappear.

DEAN: There, there.

FAK: There, there.

PATTY: I feel sick.

FAK: You going to be sick?

PATTY: No, it's all right.

DEAN: Put this round you.

FAK: (*taking off his jacket*). Here, let her have mine. What happened to you?

PATTY: What happened to you?

FAK: I dunno.

DEAN: Never mind that now, how you feeling?

PATTY: Oh, better than I was . . . oh it was awful. All alone in the dark, I never been alone in the dark before, not in the real dark . . . I never been really alone in the dark ever. (*Starting to cry again.*)

(CONE *begins to throw his dice with more violence.*)

FAK: (*holding* PATTY *and comforting her, she gradually quietens*). There, there.

PATTY: Is it all right to keep this a bit?

FAK: Yeah.

PATTY: It's nice talking.

FAK: Yeah.

PATTY: All friendly and warm.

FAK: Yeah.

PATTY: Perhaps I was stupid—just stupid—made it all up eh? Just silly! Silly! Nothing at all, nothing, and there was I all scared of nothing.

FAK: Yeah.

PATTY: Oh no it weren't nothing, I know it weren't.

FAK: Cor did you see them? Did you? Thousands— well dozens. Where'd they all come from? Oh he's been at it, Pampinato has, Pampinato's been about—where's the police I'd like to know, where's the bloody coppers?

(DEAN *takes up the dice and throws them.*)

Pacing the area they was coshing the lot, blimey! And back of the Regal—fair made your hair curl, that noisy. And some feller hanging from a lamp-post—

(CONE *takes up the dice and throws them.*)

coshing them from above—whack! With a bottle. And they grabbed the post and chucked him in the canal, lamp an' all.

(CONE *and* DEAN *are throwing the dice alternately.*)

What you playing for eh? Three five. What's the stakes? Two fours. Eh? Five six. Well what

72

you playing for? (DEAN *throws*.) Double six.
(*Pause*.)

CONE: First to get three?

DEAN: All right.
(*They go on throwing*.)

FAK: First to get three sixes? Five two. Eh? Six five.

DEAN: Double.

FAK: He's got two now, hasn't he? He's got two
doubles.

CONE: Double.

FAK: Double to you, four two, three dot, two fours.

CONE: Double.

FAK: Equal, two dots, two fives, three dot, four
three.
(*Enter* GRETA, *unnoticed by the others who are
absorbed*.)

PATTY: Hey . . .
(*Pause*.)

GRETA: What you staring at, Yank?

DEAN: I'm wondering whether your hair is natural—
Limey.

CONE: Greta!

GRETA: And what conclusion have you reached?

DEAN: It grows out of your head——

GRETA: Oh yes?

DEAN: And each Friday you dip it in blood—in human
blood.

GRETA: In babies' blood.

DEAN: In cold blood.

CONE: Stop, stop it.

DEAN: Tell me something of yourself, ma'am.

GRETA: I was born in Australia, on the other side of the
world, upside down.

DEAN: Indeed?

73

GRETA: I was reared in a cave by a female wallaby. Until I was seven I ran about on all fours and barked. Tell me something of yourself.

DEAN: My childhood was humdrum. I live off cans and gum.

GRETA: You eat tin?

DEAN: Any kind of sheet metal. I watch so much television I flicker. What's happening out there?

GRETA: You can get away if you're afraid.

DEAN: I'm not afraid.

GRETA: Well you bloody well should be.

CONE: (*furious*). Kant! Kant! Bloody cow! Go on gabber! Stand there cool, dead cool, filthy cow! Filthy cow! Filthy cow!

GRETA: (*silencing* CONE *with howls*). Ow! Ow! Ow! Ahooer! Ahooer! Ahooer! (*Pause.*) Ah that's better, anybody got a cigarette?

FAK: What'll we do now?

GRETA: Have a bit of peace.

DEAN: You sure are an extraordinary creature.

GRETA: Break me up and see how I tick.

FAK: Let's get out eh? Let's get after them. A real scrap, bash 'em off.

GRETA: No. I can't be bothered.

CONE: Why? Why can't you be bothered?

GRETA: Oh buzz.

CONE: Why can't you——

GRETA: Somebody else.

CONE: ——Be bothered? What's the matter? What's the matter with you?

GRETA: (*at* CONE). Flywheels, gasometers, chimney stacks, coal dust / newspapers, oranges, broken glass / stair-carpet, raincoats, geysers / cigarettes, cinemas. Ah! Ah! / Sausages, bedsteads, rag and iron merchants / basements, cement, up and down / Metropolitan, Bakerloo, Piccadilly / forty-seven, fifty-six, four. Ah! Ah!

DEAN: All flaying claws: ten legs like a lobster.

GRETA: Grab me in the small of the back.

DODO: Blutter the wind, blutter the wind, blutter the wind—no, it's cold . . .

(DEAN *goes to* DODO.)

CONE: (*going to her wanting to resume their relationship*). Greta . . . Greta . . .

GRETA: Oh get off. Leave me alone.

FAK: What's happening eh? Shall I do my conjuring trick?

CONE: Oh, shut up.

FAK: What are we hanging about for? When are our lot coming? When are we going to do something?

CONE: Ask her.

FAK: Hey! Hey! Where's our lot? . . . I'm fed up with this cop. I feel like a skate on a slab and everybody looking at me . . . why can't she say something? Why can't she bloody well answer?

CONE: Come over here.

PATTY: What?

CONE: You keep out of this.

FAK: What's the idea?

CONE: (*making sure that* GRETA *can hear*). Notice anything?

FAK: No, what?

CONE: With——

FAK: With?

CONE: With——

FAK: With her?

CONE: Yes.

75

FAK: What?

CONE: Well?

FAK: Nothing's happening.

CONE: Well?

FAK: She's slipping!

CONE: Well?

FAK: It's that bloody yank—I'll do him.

CONE: You're bright, aren't you?

FAK: What?

CONE: Real bright.

FAK: Oh, I wouldn't say that.

CONE: Seems a pity——

FAK: What?

CONE: A bright chap like you——

FAK: What d'you mean "It's a pity"?

CONE: No chance——

FAK: For what?

CONE: Getting no credit.

FAK: No credit?

CONE: Good looks, intelligence, personality——

FAK: Eh?

CONE: Most popular feller in town.

FAK: Oh, go on!

CONE: (*to audience*). You say so? Yes! He is!

FAK: Cor!

CONE: All you do.

FAK: I do?

CONE: That's right!

FAK: Yes, I do!

CONE: People like you are wanted.

FAK: What for?

CONE: What'll happen now——

FAK: Now?

CONE: To the fellers——

FAK: Eh?

CONE: Now she's——

FAK: Now she's——

CONE: Now she's——

FAK: Now she's washed up? That's it! Let's get at
the yank!

CONE: Someone with guns, brains, personality . . .

FAK: You mean?

CONE: Well?

FAK: You mean I could be . . .

CONE: You could be.

FAK: King of the Teds!

CONE: King of the Teds!

FAK: King of the Teds!

CONE: (*to the audience*). Meet the King of the Teds!
. . . The King of the Teds . . . who else is as
sensational, as strong, as stupid.

FAK: Tony Curtis the second.

CONE: All the fellers who've had a bash. All the
fellers with cigars and girls and gats.

FAK: King! King! King Fak! I'll put bloody south
London in fear of Fak—I'll—I'll——

CONE: Look.

FAK: What?

CONE: That.

FAK: Her?

CONE: Get outside.

FAK: I get outside.

CONE: Find one of them.

FAK: I find one of them.

CONE: Tell 'em she's here.

FAK: I tell 'em she's here . . . tell them she's here?

CONE: They'll break the place to get her and then
they'll break her and that'll be that about that.

FAK: I get outside, I find one of them . . . I tell him
she's here . . . (*his knees knocking*) what? . . .
What?

CONE: What's the matter?

FAK: 'Fraid of what she'll do.

CONE: What'll she do when she hears all this?

FAK: What?

CONE: When I tell——

FAK: You tell her? . . . What? . . . But you won't,
you——

CONE: Won't I?

FAK: What are you going to do?

CONE: What do you think?

FAK: Wait.

CONE: No waits.

FAK: I'll—I'll——

CONE: What.

FAK: Go.

CONE: Good.

PATTY: I heard every word you said! Every—you
should be ashamed of yourself—and you! What
d'you think you're doing? What'll you get from
her? What'll you get from him?

FAK: Oh.

CONE: Shut up. Shut up, you silly little bitch.

PATTY: Shut you, you cheeky beast. (*To* FAK) Listen
you? You're getting a job, steady. Ten pounds a
week regular and furnish on the never-never.

FAK: Ten pounds——

PATTY: Ten pounds regular.

PATTY: And if I keep on at the stores——

FAK: Keep on——

PATTY: We'll go to the flicks and Palais and there'll be
television and we might have a bit of garden

78

and the weeks'll be Monday to Saturday and
we'll have the tele and go dancing sometimes
and we'll never get into debt except on the
never-never but that's different and oh! You'll
do what you're told, what's good for you and
there'll be covers on the chairbacks and table
mats and china condiments and hot water and
electricity. Come on! Before somebody stops us
or hurts us. Let's get off! Let's get off! They're
different! They can stand it—you don't know,
you can't see, but quick! Quick! So I don't
have to see!

CONE: Get off! Get off! You can't hide! They'll find
you! They'll get you.

(*Exit* PATTY *and* FAK.)

Dodo! . . . Soft . . . all looking after
themselves . . . nobody takes any . . . you.
What d'you think you're doing, eh? Garry.
Pampinato. Fak. Fak! What about Fak?—eh?
Fak's splitting—he told me! He's getting you!
He's going to tell Pampi-potato you're here! I
heard him! The Potato'll come and he'll tear!
Tear! After what you did he'll kill you! Take
some notice of me! Take some notice of me!
. . . Somebody do something about me . . .
What does she think she is? . . . What does she
think? . . . Oh, it don't matter to me . . . I'm
not—I'm not taking any . . . bitch! Bitch! Silly
fat bitch! Sow! . . . Sow! . . . Sow! Sow! Sow!
What about me? . . . Stop me! Stop me! Stop
me and buy one! (*Weeping*) All right. All right.
I'm going—I'm going to find him and tell him.
I'll tell him about Ronny and Gerry and
Connie—he'll wreck you. He'll wreck you!

79

Break! Rip! Crack! Tear! And it'll be you! I'll
tell Pampinato and he'll destroy you. The sky'll
be black and purple and the blood'll knot in
the veins and it'll be you! You! I'll destroy
you! I'll destroy earth! I'll destroy everything!
And it'll be you! You! You! You! You!
(CONE *hits* GRETA *like an angry, resentful child
wishing to draw attention to itself but not daring
to hit hard and not having the strength. As he
hits her the quality of his touching changes. He
realizes that she is pregnant. A very long pause.
If possible play without words otherwise add in*
CONE: *You won't want me any more.*
Exit CONE. *Offstage three terrible howls each
farther away in the distance.*)

DEAN: Why did you let Cone go like that?
GRETA: Oh are you still here? What did you say?
DEAN: Why did you let Cone go like that?
GRETA: Well run along, there's a good chap. Just at this
moment I can't be bothered with you.
DEAN: I want to talk to you. No seriously. Someone's
got to talk to you.
GRETA: Here and now? With that lot out there? Are you
crazy? They won't leave us long, you know,
they'll be coming.
DEAN: The fact that they are coming doesn't worry
me.
GRETA: It will, it will.
DEAN: I don't care about dying, or being hurt—or
rather there are things which concern me much
more.
GRETA: You're a drag.
DEAN: We won't talk about me.
GRETA: There's nothing hurts more than being hurt.

80

DEAN: We'll talk about you. Why did you let Cone go?

GRETA: Let's not talk about that now.

DEAN: Yes we will.

GRETA: It's none of your business.

DEAN: The human race is my business.

GRETA: Mr. Big Business.

DEAN: It's not decent. He trusted you, relied on you, lived for you. How can you just turn him off? Don't you see? Strong people have a responsibility towards weak people. If the strong don't help the weak where will it end? It's back to chaos. Looking at it even from the meanest angle of self-interest: if you're a strong person you must help weak people, you must look after old people, for instance. In your own interest you must establish it as a social habit, part of the morals of civilized society that the young and strong protect the weak and old. One day you yourself will be weak and old and then the social law you have made will be your protection.

(GRETA *is in pain.*)

I'm sorry . . . I'm sorry . . . Let me help you . . . is there anything I can do? Let me fetch someone—a doctor—I'm sure I could find a doctor—you ought to be in hospital—let me take you to——

GRETA: No, no not likely, leave me alone . . . go on talking, just go on talking.

(*Pause.*)

DEAN: But that's putting it at its meanest level. There is a far more moral reason why you should protect Cone, why the strong should protect

81

the weak: to act otherwise is below human dignity—don't you see? Every time anyone does anything cruel or immoral—and I don't mean moral in the sexual sense but in its widest sense, moral behaviour in the sense of trying to act with love and truth in all you do—every time anyone does anything cruel or immoral he betrays mankind. I'm not a religious person, at least I'm not a Christian, a churchgoer, but this is what I feel—I can't see any reason for men being on this earth, but since we are here, we men, we must try and become better, we must seek to become better and better, to help to create order, truth and love. It's so easy to slide into chaos—don't you see that? You're intelligent and strong—surely you understand —yes?

GRETA: Eh? What did you say? (*Pause.*) Look, if you don't mind I think I'll toddle along, it's all ever so interesting and thanks ever so but er——

DEAN: I want you to listen to me.

GRETA: Some other time, yes?

DEAN: Stay where you are.

GRETA: Eh?

DEAN: You heard me that time.

GRETA: Fat lot I care.

DEAN: It's obscene, it's obscene. You care nothing for life, for cherishing life, for love, friendship. You're disgusting. Disgusting! Just tearing life down and trampling on it. Reverence for life! Reverence for life! The things you kill can never, never! Be replaced. It's disgusting! It's totally obscene! Agh!

GRETA: Oh friend that worries me, that really worries me.

DEAN: I don't care if it worries you! I don't give a damn! You're going to hear. Somebody's got to get it into that thick cruel skull. Don't interrupt me! No self-control! No discipline! What's a world without serenity, without mutual assurance, a bedrock of mutual trust, of laws and decencies you can rely on? Be quiet! All the things decent men have striven for, all the high aims: learning, philosophy, morality, and I don't mean sexual morality, I mean total morality: moral discipline, a moral philosophy of responsibility that each man hammers out for himself and tries to live by.

GRETA: For crying out loud, I'm off——

DEAN: You're not.

GRETA: I am.

(GRETA *starts to go, he pulls her down.*)

DEAN: You're stopping.

GRETA: Rough stuff.

DEAN: Yes.

GRETA: Just you remember it's a pregnant woman you're pulling around.

DEAN: Pregnant! Pregnant woman! You pregnant! You're not fit to have a child. What'll your child be? What'll it's life be?

GRETA: Rough.

DEAN: You're disgusting! You destroy people. You eat them, you eat them. A boy, your friend, trusts you, and you just toss him off: "Go away, I'm sick of you." You obscenity! You gross thing! Man/woman, cruel! Unstable! Frigid!

83

GRETA : Frigid?

DEAN : Yes frigid! No love, no true morality, no giving, all taking! You eat men, you eat them, well, you shan't eat me! You shan't devour me! You and your kind—how dare you? Look at me! Look at me! What have you got to say? What have you got to say? You! You! You! Dragging us down, down to your level! Crawling, ferreting among the muck, muck! And you know what I mean don't you? Muck! You filthy-minded, vicious! You know it! You glory in it! Glory! Glory! Glory! Look at me! Look at me! This is the first time, the first time you've had it, had it strong and true, and the first time, yes. And me? I'm telling you, you. I'm telling—giving it to you straight, straight and strong. Look at me! You look at me, straight, straight, at someone giving it you! Yes sister! Giving it you for the first time—the first time—and it's me!

(GRETA *in pain which carries forward to her lines at the end of his speech.*)

Me! I'm the one that's giving it you! D'you hear? Me! Straight and strong you're getting it, getting for the first and it's me that's giving it you, me giving it straight and strong——

GRETA : Strong—strong.

DEAN : Yes strong——

GRETA : But them—the fight—the bash——

DEAN : Bash—bash—lash——

GRETA : Lash——

DEAN : Whiplash! Whiplash! Whiplash and suck, suck—sucks you down.

GRETA : Sucks down——

84

DEAN: Down—running loose——

GRETA: Running loose—hah hah!

DEAN: Come with me! Come! Come!

GRETA: Lash!

DEAN: Come! Come with me!

GRETA: Lash! Lash!

DEAN: You're coming! You're coming with me if I have to knock you out, knock knock! I just don't care—I just don't—I'll kill—kill——

GRETA: Lash!

DEAN: Kill—It's going to kill——

GRETA: Lash!

DEAN: Kill you kill——

GRETA: Kill——

DEAN: Kill——

GRETA: Bang! I'm dying, I'm in the throes of death! Bang! Bang! Feel! Feel! Bang! Bang! (*Holding* DEAN *by the hair.*) Try and beat me! Try and eat me! Hah! Look at you! You're so weak you can't stand, you'll fall, you're falling. You can't come you can't go. What are you? A whisp of will, a thread of pride, a sigh of thought.

DEAN: Dodo! Dodo! Help me!
(DODO *runs away and exits.*)
The gun! Where's the gun?

GRETA: You want to kill me? Not likely, I'm not going to die before I have to.

DEAN: It's for me, it's for me.

GRETA: Oh go and get rid of yourself, I want to settle with this bastard.
(*An explosion off.*)
Listen! Listen you! Cocky! Pipe down! Listen quick—no no be quiet a minute . . . a moment

—just a moment—oh. This interlocking, intertwining, interliving—friendship? Love? Huh! Oh bloody organic confusion . . . Oh you! Oh you! Oh . . . Oh . . . Oh . . . just here . . . (*Pause.*) . . . (*Pause.*) . . . (*A long pause.*) . . . Now I let this child into life. . . . Now I thrust this bird into the air . . .

(*Machine-gun fire off. Enter* FAK *carrying a large white sheet and* PATTY *sketchily dressed up as a nurse and carrying a large book entitled "How To Deliver A Baby".* STEVE *rams a wig on his head, picks up a banjo, which he holds like a tommy-gun, and comes on raking the auditorium with his "gun".*)

STEVE: (*to audience*). Stay where you are. This is a stick-up. O.K. where is she?

GRETA: Pampinato!

STEVE: My aboriginee love! Little one, why did you never tell?

GRETA: I've been a fool, a fool, is it too late?

STEVE: Never say those words "too late". (*To audience*) One cheep out of you lot and I'll flash you. (FAK *and* PATTY *hold up the sheet and* GRETA *goes behind.*)
What are you doing behind there?

GRETA: What do you think? Lucky you came in time.

STEVE: But you can't do that! It's not nice, not customary, not legal.

GRETA: Rails, rules, laws, guides, promises, terms, guarantees, conventions, traditions: into the pot with the whole bloody lot. Birth! Birth! That's the thing! Oh, I shall have hundreds of children, millions of hundreds and hundreds of millions.

86

STEVE: We'll see about that.

FAK: (*to* PATTY). And shall we be happy, very, very happy?

PATTY: Ooh! You should just see what it says here.

FAK: But they grow under gooseberry bushes . . . don't they?

(*Infant cries from behind the sheet. Sheet falls to reveal* GRETA *and a small white bundle.*)

STEVE: It might be mine, it looks like me . . . it must be mine.

(*A distant cry. Pause.*)

GRETA: What happened to Cone?

FAK: Dead.

GRETA: How did he die?

FAK: He bashed himself to death with a brick. He rubbed himself out.

(*Pause.* DEAN *rises and looks at* GRETA. *Exit* DEAN.)

STEVE: (*to audience*). O.K. you lot, clear out. I'm blowing this place up. We'll have a bonfire: bring your own axes. All right everyone off! Off! (*To* GRETA) And you keep out of mischief—or else . . .

(*Exit* STEVE, FAK *and* PATTY. GRETA *examines the "baby" with lively interest.*)

(*Slow fade.*)

(*The End*)